THE LONG RIDE

D.M. WOOLSTON

VIRGINIA VAN PELT

THE LONG RIDE

First edition. May 31, 2022.

ISBN: 978-0986144363

Written by D.M. Woolston.

CONTENTS

For my Aunt Virginia, who taught me the wonder of the night sky.

ACKNOWLEDGMENTS

'The Long Ride' was a gift, given to me by my first cousin Linda Monk, who's mom, Virginia Van Pelt, had begun writing in the 1960's but had not completed.

I accepted the gift, graciously, and wondered if I would ever be up to the challenge of becoming a co-writer with the Aunt I had grown up with, but had since gone back to the Lord.

Aunt Virginia was always kind to me. I enjoyed her innate sense of wonder about the universe we live in. My dad, Robert, her brother, has that too.

Writing this story was harder than I thought it would be, but more rewarding than I could have imagined. The process of writing Historical Fiction was new to me, and so I've learned a great deal about what it takes to research worlds of the past.

I hope, dear reader, that you enjoy this story. May it transport you back to the time of the Old West where one's self reliance was key, and the tough skills needed for physical survival were tested daily.

D.M. Woolston

NEW IN TOWN

*M*ilborne left the bar after two shots of whisky. The crowd had already become raucous, and he thought it best not to partake in the fun. Besides, he had an early morning job so an example needed setting. His men, Dobbs, Gate, and Buckshot, were still throwing a few back. He had faith, though, that they'd soon steer clear of the party like he did. Their hides would be in as much jeopardy as his if they failed their orders. So far he'd been able to trust that his towering lieutenant, Dobbs, would keep the other two in line.

A breeze rustled through the trees as Milborne walked along the dark and dusty Mexican street, back to the hostel where he and his crew were holdup for the last few days. The nearly full moon spread a good portion of pale light on the wooden buildings, making up the small town of Xochimilco, south of Mexico City.

While passing the front of a mercantile, he heard a scuffling from up around the corner and then the muffled sound of a woman's cry. He pressed himself up against the building and peered around the corner into the alleyway. There, in the dim light, he saw two men who had her pinned against a wall.

"Come on sweetheart, you know you wanna—"

Milborne left the light of the street and advanced into the alley, disappearing into the same shadows. He drew his double-action revolver, cocking the hammer back with a click.

"You yellows have about two seconds before I make some new holes in ya."

The outlines of two dark figures spun on their heels and high-tailed it. The woman slumped to the ground, sobbing.

Milborne approached her. "Listen... I ain't gonna hurt ya, but you can't stay here by yerself. Too much goings' on so near the cantina."

She cried a soft thank you and scrambled away, in the opposite direction of her attackers.

He holstered the gun. It was the same old thing; enter a town, frequent the watering holes to learn who's who, then assist the local authorities as needed. He had a natural ability to shoot, but didn't like to do it much. Unfortunately, he had a heap of practice over the last few years of riding as a Rurales.

Running the small detachment as their captain had its perks. Like a fine LeMat Revolver and a genuine beaver-felt hat. But as time wore on, Milborne wearied of the work. Rurales were judge, jury, and executioner on the open range. Riding as a lightweight team on broncos and serving up instant justice.

He wanted to quit, but options were scarce. Ever since leaving the United States with a price on his head, he'd fled to Mexico and found work under the growing political instability of the president Diaz administration. The Mexican army was having a hard time keeping the peace, so the Rurales were established. But rebellious tejanos continued to fight back against a government who took their land.

Milborne thought pretty high of himself to hide from the Mexican authorities right under their noses as a hired gun. He thought being a Rurales would be the perfect cover to keep from being found out as a wanted man from America. As the unrest got worse, however, he wound up working closer and closer alongside the Mexican Army. It made him nervous every time they called upon his small regiment to round up more rebels and put them in prison. Milborne preferred to stay on the free side of those dead-end bars.

On the way back to the hostel to bed for the night, Milborne pondered his orders. The job was risky, as usual. They gave him and his crew the task of capturing a rebel along with his supposedly stolen silver coined double-eagles.

EARLY NEXT MORNING, Milborne had the wagon all set near a small dock, away from the chiefly used part of the river. The tangled shoreline of thick shrubs and trees made a perfect place to hide in wait for the rendezvous. He used to be a wagon driver in the states, too, except he worked for a small company called Wells Fargo.

The job back then was legitimate. It required him to drive a well-secured wagon in the transfer of cash and sometimes precious metals from one bank to another. It was steady work, but also dangerous as holdups were bound to occur. He'd get paid immediately after the run, lose most of it on cards, then have to go back to work. Occasionally he even spent some on the ladies at the watering hole, but no chance of marriage ever came of it.

After an hour Milborne became impatient. This was the place they agreed upon. Did he miss something? There'd be hell to pay if he had gotten the orders wrong. The penny paper it was written on had long been consumed by the fire he'd thrown it into after committing to memory.

High season had come to the river. Milborne spied many boats wading by, loaded with partygoers or mariachis playing loud music. Most of the shallow boats had a makeshift cabin section near the middle, created by draping colorfully decorated cloth over a simple wooden frame. The drivers plunging their long poles into the waterway to navigate much like the gondoliers of Venice.

Eventually, Milborne saw a boat break away from the pack and head in his direction. Gate was steering the boat, so he figured that Dobbs, Buckshot, and their prisoner were inside the cabin.

When the boat reached the dock, Dobbs emerged with the bound and gagged prisoner. He had a streak of dried blood on his face but he was conscious. Gate quickly helped him move the man from the boat to Milborne's wagon. After that, both men went back inside and came out carrying a leather satchel. The coins landed with a clank as they slung the heavy bag into the back of the wagon next to their silent captive.

"There's a hefty sum of silver in there," Dobbs said. "Good thing we got him before the scum could use it to aid those revolutionaries."

"Where's Buckshot?" Milborne asked, realizing he should've been there, too.

"We lost him," Dobbs replied. "Hazards of the job, I guess," he added coolly. Without warning, both men boarded their boat and pushed away from the shore.

"I thought you guys were riding with me?" Milborne asked.

"Naaah, you can handle it," Gate replied. "We have to ditch this thing to keep our cover from the rebels."

"We'll meet you at the jailhouse," Dobbs called back.

It wasn't the plan, but Milborne now held both the silver and the prisoner. He tied down a heavy tarp that completely covered the open back of the wagon. All this cash on him now. Just like in the states. Except he had much more autonomy south of the line. Heck, he could probably disappear and get away with it.

He steered the two horses away from the river, easing the wagon along a dirt trail. No hurry. He didn't want to arouse any attention. The next stop was in town to hand the prisoner and the money over to the local police. The temptation to take the money run was there. But he never stole the money back then and would not do it here.

After crossing a small bridge along the trail, four men on horses came out of nowhere and surrounded him. The Federales had their guns drawn. Barrels pointing at Milborne's chest.

WELCOME TO BELEM

*B*ound at both wrists and ankles, Milborne endured the short ride in the back of his own wagon. Hooves rattled on stone when they entered the streets of Mexico City. At last they arrived at what seemed the oldest building he'd ever seen. Even though the mass of stonework was three stories tall, he'd been ushered down a stairwell and locked in a damp cell in the basement. Milborne had done nothing wrong, and yet his payoff was a sentence in the dark, foul-smelling dungeons of Belem.

Besides three walls of scarred stone and a singular hole in the floor smelling of feces, the bars faced another solid wall of a hallway. Sounds of a prisoner being beaten and most likely a laughing guard echoed from elsewhere. After an hour

Milborne called for one. The guard came around wearing a stained and ratty uniform.

"So, what's the easiest way out of here," Milborne asked, hoping it would get him a laugh instead of a beating.

The guard replied with a wry grin, "Death, senor."

～

MILBORNE LOST weight as the days went on. Still, nobody would tell him anything.

Days ticked by in anguish as he wondered what happened to his crew. Many days later, a visitor stopped at the other side of the iron bars to his stinking cell.

"Good to see you, senor. I trust your accommodations are acceptable?"

"What the hell Dobbs... why am I here?"

Dobbs leaned with his back against the opposite wall, striking a match. "Things have changed. Haven't you heard?" He lit a rolled cigarette and took a deep draw.

"What are you talking about?"

"In case you didn't know, yesterday, November 10th, will go down in history. Francisco Madero's insurrection was a success. Even Diaz and his men are on the run. Vive la Mexico, hey? You are but a peon of the old establishment now."

Milborne tried to recall the lost days. It had been nearly two months in this hellhole. "Why imprison me?" Milborne asked.

"It's my turn to be captain, and the commandant agrees. You can rot here where you belong."

Milborne slumped against a wall, slick with mold. He couldn't stand being fenced in like this. Someone in the states had already made him take the fall for a bank robbery he had no hand in. Now again, getting framed for doing another honest day's work. He must be a real sucker to let this happen twice. Maybe he should've never gone out west, and instead worked at his father's business back in New York City. But textiles bored Milborne to death. No way he could ever cope with being chained to a desk. He grasped the bars in front of him. "You bastard. Who else was in on it?"

Dobbs tilted his hat back a bit and scratched a wooly sideburn. "Let's see here. Gate was on board, but Buckshot... well, we didn't see eye to eye." He clicked his tongue and shot at Milborne's head pretending his hand was a gun. "So long, amigo."

Dobbs walked away, looking like a man without a care in the world. Of the whole group Milborne had the bad luck of working with, Dobbs was the most ruthless. He was also the type of man who, whenever he found a gun in his hand, felt compelled to use it.

Still, Milborne wasn't sure what to believe about Madero's uprising. He needed information from the outside. Of what he understood so far, Diaz welcomed elites of countries like the United States and France to buy up the land. When a desirable plot wouldn't sell, he'd force the locals into slave labor or kick them off the land they had long toiled to call home.

He knew trouble had been brewing for some time. Heck, his job was because of it. He had nothing against the rebels for fighting against their worsening poverty. Milborne was done with the Rurales.

Another meaningless day ended, and he fell asleep. That is until the noise of someone getting beaten roused him. Guards rushed by his bars and soon the screaming turned to muffled cries. Milborne kicked himself for not leaving Mexico sooner. He'd go through Hell's fire before rotting inside a greaser prison. He had to be free, and if death was the only way, so be it.

LEY DE FUGA

The next morning two guards hauled Milborne out of his cell. They took him up the stairs to a large courtyard, stripped him naked, then doused him with a few cold buckets of water. Eventually the filth that was wedged into every body crevice washed away.

"Now you are good enough to see the commandant," one of his handlers said.

They led Milborne up to the ground floor and into an office of sorts, then they pushed him into the small jailed-off section in the room's corner. Another prisoner was in the cell already, looking like they had handled him the same way as Milborne. Still damp from the hard washing.

After the guards locked him behind the bars, they left the office and closed its heavy wooden door. The jailing area occupied a few square feet of a much larger room containing a wooden desk and chairs. One wall displayed an enormous map of Mexico City. A corked whiskey bottle sat on the desk.

The two men were alone. The prisoner glanced at the closed door of the room, then he reached through the bars and caressed the ancient-looking padlock.

"This piece of trash... I could pick it right now. Eh?"

Milborne shook his head. "I wouldn't do that."

"We escape or die," The man whispered. "Now is the chance... but it would be better with the both of us."

Milborne shook his head. There was an uneasiness about the stranger's demeanor. Twitching muscles bespoke of the man's desperation. Milborne knew enough of this type of behavior that he himself had to remain vigil, for his own safety.

The prisoner gazed at the dusty street through the iron bars and out a nearby window. Beyond the street lay an open field of scrub grass. "But I must get out. I must!"

"Sorry, but we each gotta face the repercussions of our actions. And I need to ask the commandant what action justifies my being here."

A hearty but quiet laugh burst from the man. He pulled out a metal rod from somewhere and reached through the bars, inserting it into the gaping hole of the bulky lock. Within seconds, the lock gave way with a low click as it fell open.

"There is no reason for us to be here, senor. The commandant is corrupt."

Before Milborne knew what was happening, the man eased the bars open and disappeared quietly out the office door. Could it be that easy? Maybe the man was right. Maybe he should've left too. A chance like this may not come again.

Two guards rushed into the office. Milborne recognized one of them as a previous guard, but the other man wore a crisp uniform and held the air of authority. The familiar guard shut the cell's iron-bar door and quickly re-clasped the lock. The other man, who was obviously in charge, walked over behind the desk and sat in the chair. "Welcome to the Prison of Belem. I am Sanchez Noriega, your commandant. Now please, look out the window."

Milborne peered through the bars at the outside world. The man who escaped had just fled across the street, and now he headed for a low set of hills in the distance. A single gunshot rang out as the man stumbled, then lay motionless.

The commandant opened the bottle on the desk, then drank off the rest of his whiskey. He sighed while putting both feet up on his desk. "I see you are the smarter one."

Milborne recalled that some unfortunate souls, like the man who was just murdered, won the quick merciful death of the Ley de Fuga, or lynch law. The law was supposed to empower police to shoot escaping prisoners, but in practice it became a quick way to execute a man who no longer had value. After making him think he'd escaped, by law they could fill him with lead.

"Why am I here?" Milborne asked.

"Because, you tried to steal the rebels' money from us."

"I did no such thing. I was on my way to deliver the prisoner and the money to the authorities in Xochimilco."

"Your fellows tell a different story," Sanchez said, "They said you were tired of it all, and that you planned on taking the money and leaving."

"I was bringing him in," Milborne said through his teeth.

"I don't think so," the commandant quickly replied. He stood while resting both palms flat on his desk. "You were going to dump the rebel, that's why you left him tied up. And you took the silver. In my book, they call that stealing."

"I was framed. And you know it. Dobbs told me as much. Now, what is the real reason you have me here?"

"You want to know why, gringo? For robbing the First Bank in El Paso, and for murdering the bank teller, of course."

TIME TO GO

*M*ilborne eased back on the stained bench of the cell. The bank robbery he had no part in had finally caught up with him. "I didn't shoot that teller!"

Sanchez waved a hand in dismissal. "I enlisted your Dobbs to set you up, but I didn't tell him of the price on your head. You are too valuable to me. Besides, our new presidente Maduro cannot overlook any source of revenue. The revolt has been costly, and when we discovered that you already have a sizable price on your head in your own country, well, I really had no choice."

The portly commandant of Belem stood and walked over to the large map hanging on the wall. He set a fat finger onto it near the town of Chihuahua. "You'll be escorted to a much nicer prison near the northern border. Es over eight-hundred miles, so be careful of snakes." He winked at Milborne and went to the doorway.

Milborne thought of how much more dangerous it was in Mexico now that a new president wanted things his own way. There'd be more blood in the streets before long. He should've taken his chances and stayed back in the states, gone into hiding years ago. Too late, though. He'd get an escort all the way up north. No way to get anywhere on his own accord now.

"Well, I have to go," Sanchez said. "Please remember, you are smarter than the man who stood next to you a few minutes ago. But my men, they will not give you the easy way out with a bullet in the back."

Chuckling to himself, the commandant left Milborne alone with his thoughts and regrets; of which he had many.

LATER THAT DAY, Milborne found himself bound tight at the wrists and ankles. They placed him into the back of an open wagon for the transfer up north. Another prisoner was already there, bound as well. A younger man. Bruises in many places.

The driver, whose only name was Cookie, clucked at the horses and started them away from the prison. Two other guards on broncos flanked them.

As they trotted along a road leading out of the city, Milborne noticed a man tied to a high wooden cross, crucified. Around the neck hung a sign with 'Traitor to the Future' emblazoned on it. Yep, a new president is full of new solutions.

One guard on horseback pointed his Winchester repeater at the dead man up high on the cross. "There before the grace of God go you... senors." Ramirez said. He was the oldest of the men, and Milborne pegged him as the boss of the trio, given his age and air of authority.

The young man tied up next to Milborne stirred but did not speak. Milborne thought to introduce himself. Maybe it would help him forget the pain of his body and disheartening situation. "Name's Milborne."

"Miguel," he replied. His voice had a gravelly sound. The boy wasn't well. After speaking with him a while, Milborne learned that the young man was from a wealthy family, and that he'd wound up with a huge gambling debt until thrown into prison.

The wagon lurched side to side every so often, causing the two men to collide and recover. Crossing eight hundred miles, they'd have to put up with twenty some odd more days of this. The caravan halted after a full day of travel. Milborne imagined that at the end of the journey his captures would receive a handsome payment, while Milborne himself would receive the end of a rope. It was too much to dwell on for long. That night he fell asleep on a blanket on the ground, where he was told not to stray from. They fed him beans before bedding down, but he was still malnourished from having to endure the last several months of decay in the dungeons of Belem.

At first light, Milborne woke up with a start. The third guard, named Tiny, hovering over him, pistol drawn, aimed at Milborne's gut. The man wore a sombrero, and based on what the driver had mentioned when they were being loaded up, the short man had a mean streak a mile long.

Milborne froze. His hands and feet were still tied so there wasn't much he could do against a gun at point blank range. Maybe they changed their minds and didn't want to make the difficult journey? Or maybe new orders were to simply kill him and move on.

Tiny yanked the trigger. The loud bang echoed in Milborne's ears as he tasted gun-smoke. Looking over, he saw the dead rattlesnake on the ground next to him. It would be another very long day.

ON THE ROAD

en days of travel passed under the burning sun. The hot fireball in the sky intent on consuming the last bit of moisture in every living thing. He and Miguel would get their hands untied for lunch and supper, but have to sleep bound at both wrists and ankles. At least it proved both their value as prisoners.

Milborne saw himself as no longer possessing any of the requisites for gregarious living. He trusted his back to no man. As for simple run-of-the-mill things like talking, laughing, exchanging horseplay, it seemed an eternity since he'd indulged in anything except the talk required to enact slaughter, or the hedging with words required to stay alive. As for his physical appearance, he doubted there would be anything reassuring to a stranger. Regardless of all that, Milborne felt he must at least try to recruit the young man for his help. "I'm going to escape," he whispered. "Are you with me?"

Miguel shot a glance over at the guards unpacking to prepare for the evening meal. "No senor, I cannot. My father is a wealthy hidalgo and will pay for my release when we get there. He has a wonderful hacienda near the border. Maybe when you get free, you can come and stay?"

"I can't. They plan on sending me back to the states to hang."

Miguel nodded.

Milborne would go it alone, but he built a hope that the kid would be alright. The sun dipped below the horizon, shedding waves of reds and yellows across the high clouds of the west. Darkness would have been best, but Milborne knew it had to be now, despite the overpowering odds against him. Waiting for the rare moment when his hands would be free for the last meal of the day, he used one of the oldest tricks in the book. He spread the cook fire.

It caught quickly to the dry brush. Milborne angled out of sight while the flames took everyone's focus. He made it to the horses and located a knife in the saddlebag, using it to make quick work of the reins that he didn't have time to untie. Smartly, he left enough length to keep control when riding.

In a desperate jump for the saddle, Milborne fell short because of his impaired muscles. They would not respond the way they used to. Pulling himself up with all his might, he mounted and flew into a gallop. Yells came from close behind. They could only give chase with the wagon and the Ramirez's bronco.

If the sun had been low on the horizon, at least it would have provided a chance for keeping sunlight in the eyes of his pursuer, but that wasn't the case. He made it maybe fifty yards before the first shot whizzed past. Must be Ramirez. Many times over the last few days, the man boasted of being an expert marksman by learning the ways of the gauchos. Right now Milborne gave little for his chances against such a shot, but there was no going back.

With the second bullet Milborne felt a white hot pain in his shoulder, causing him to career off his mount. The ground came fast as he hit hard enough to knock the wind out of him. Dirt in his mouth mixed with the bitter taste of regret.

After a few moments, Ramirez came into view. His voice echoed from overhead. "So, you think you can out-ride me, aye?"

Milborne had nothing to say, even if he wanted to. Not enough air in his lungs to try. Oddly enough, the bulk of his regret lay in not having recognized his own limitations for what they were, but in this utter failure of an escape. His consciousness fluttered away until he knew no more.

A GAME OF CARDS

Milborne's return to life revealed a carefully bandaged chest. He lay on the rough ground with vague and painful recollections of having a bullet dug out. For a time he'd forgotten how accurate some riders could shoot, his memory now refreshed.

Ramirez had put his lead right where he wanted to. High enough to bring his quarry down, but not center enough to hit any of the vital organs. If heretofore Milborne had harbored any doubts about the validity of his belief that they were saving him for something big, those doubts were gone.

The morning had come, and with it an unfamiliar ache in Milborne's shoulder. Upon getting loaded into the wagon with the prisoner Miguel, the driver turned and spoke to Milborne.

"I'm a better cook than a doctor, but you should survive a few more nights. We're almost there."

"We didn't kill you," Tiny added, "because you are like gold."

Ramirez smirked and rode past the wagon, starting another day's long ride.

That night at camp, they left Milborne's hands tied so he could not escape, and not eat. The men were drinking, celebrating their diligence in preventing the loss of a prisoner. Their game of cards became loud as more and more tequila flowed.

Eventually, Tiny stumbled over and invited them both to play. Miguel's eyes lit up as he offered his trembling hands to be untied. Milborne shook his head, saying he was too tired of losing. Then he turned to Miguel. "Do not do this, kid."

After several minutes of play, Tiny shouted, "You may be rich, but you are nothing. Tu familia es escoria! Your illegal wealth will be taken from you and given back to the people. You lived off the fat of the man from Oxcaca, but he is gone now."

Tiny pushed Miguel to the ground and began kicking him in the head with the hard-nosed tip of his boot.

Milborne bent and twisted until reaching an off-balance stance. He desperately wanted to reach Miguel and stop the punishment, but Cookie and Ramirez rushed over and grabbed their compadre, dragging him back to the campfire. After Miguel stood on his own with difficulty, he eased his way back to his blanket.

"Are you okay?" Milborne asked.

"Yeah, I think so."

But that wasn't the case. Milborne saw blood flowing down the young man's forehead and also from one ear. "Hey, Miguel's bleeding over here!"

Cookie came over and checked out the damage, wiping the blood away with the same dirty rag he used for cleaning dishes. "Looks like he'll be okay. He can't die, for chrissakes. Otherwise we won't collect our monies." He turned to Milborne, "Now, get back to your spot and bunk down."

Milborne hobbled back over to his blanket, thinking about how little their lives were worth.

A SLIGHT CHANCE

*D*ay thirty-six on the long ride marked their arrival into the town of Delicias, being about one-hundred and fifty miles from the northern border. The last four days of travel were the worst for Milborne. He awoke afterwards in some sort of recovery room. The high fever had come from infection, probably the dirty knife that Cookie had used to remove the bullet.

He recalled being separated from Miguel, and that the young man seemed okay despite being bruised up badly. Beyond that, Milborne's recollection stopped because of his convoluted state of mind.

"How are you feeling, senor?"

"Fine, I reckon."

"Then the bromine injection worked," the doctor

said. He smiled, revealing several missing teeth. His gray hair pulled back in long, fraying strands.

Milborne's shoulder still felt like a hot iron had pressed through. "Am I in jail?"

"No, senor, this is a hospital nearby. Your fever is gone, so you are fit enough to be sent over to the jail now."

Milborne normally wouldn't ask a stranger for help, but this time he resisted his prideful mind and hoped maybe the doctor would have some sympathy for his situation. "Doctor, please, I don't belong in that place. They framed me down in Mexico City. Please, is there anything you can do?"

The doctor had his back turned, working at a countertop where medical implements lay. "No. I have my orders." After a pause he raised his head and sighed, "but I am aware of your sticky situation." He turned around. "You did not mention the price on your head from the Americas."

Milborne winced at hearing it. "It's the truth, but that's another time where justice was not served."

The doctor peered outside the door and scanned the hallway. When he returned, his voice dropped low. "I can do nothing for you myself, but I can tell you the man in charge, Delgado Estanza, is a bad man. He takes advantage of all who are sent to him."

"How do you know this?" Milborne asked.

"I spend many a day patching up the bodies that

come from that place. I've never seen so many good men beaten and broken."

"And still you will not help me?"

"I am afraid, no, except to tell you there is but one man employed by Delgado who is just. His name is Hector. Tell him the snake feeds again. He may find a way to help, if he can."

"Sure, with a bullet in my back."

"No, senor, this is no trap... trust me. I feel ashamed for the wrongs so often committed there."

A nurse entered the room as the doctor resumed at normal voice level, "and a guard will be here for you within the hour."

FROM BAD TO WORSE

They blindfolded Milborne on the way over to the jail until arriving inside a large courtyard. He figured it made it harder for any prisoners to see an escape route. Soon Milborne found himself locked into a jail cell with no windows, but there were a few cracks in the aging adobe wall. The room had a hole in the floor for a toilet and two ragged cots were situated across from one another at each wall.

An oblique ray of sunlight seeped through a rent in the rough wall, saving him from total darkness. But it could not bring enough fresh air into the room to dispel the stench of the earthen floor. Everything about him was rank from the dampness. Worst of all, the smell of Belem still clung to him like an unhealthy aura.

Rising with effort, Milborne put his face up to the hole in the wall, feeling the soaked-in heat of the day's sun penetrate the tough fiber of his clothing when he pressed close enough to get a view of the outside world. Obviously, the building wasn't always a jail. Outside he saw the usual barren, sun-baked square which townfolk were want to build around. The new government must have taken residence and converted the shopping center to suit their needs. They flanked it on both sides by the same kind of squat, flat-roofed structure as the one he occupied. Windowless mostly, the buildings were now most likely the police headquarters and storage for the arsenal.

Across the square were more buildings, made up entirely of what looked like stables and blacksmith accommodations. Someone completely walled the grounds off from the town beyond, except for a narrow alley which bisected the stables. That small alleyway. It could lead to freedom.

This was not the first time during the long day that Milborne had fallen to making mental note of his surroundings, although for what purpose he had not yet decided. Escape would be challenging, considering the way they handled him so far. He suspected that when the time came for them to move him farther up North, he'd get no better treatment than he'd received on the way up from Belem.

On occasions of getting fed, a guard stood with his Henry rifle in the corridor outside. Milborne kept an ear out for the name of Hector to be mentioned, but maybe the man wasn't working there anymore. The faint chance of escape becoming an ever-increasing impossibility.

For the first time in all the long months since his capture, Milborne knew a complete sense of futility. But now here, with the outside world within range of his vision and his ultimate fate but days or perhaps only hours away, he became forced to face reality and the hopelessness of his plight. It was painfully clear that the corrupt government employees had used him as a bargaining chip, as completely and cleverly as all the others who were rotting away in places like this. Probably he had known it all along, but hadn't dared allow himself to believe it down there in the darkness, otherwise he would have gone mad.

At least for now he regained his senses, but staying locked up for the rest of his life is what he feared most of all. Let them do their damndest now. He was ready for them. They had reduced him to a shadow of his former physical self. A half-starved, grimy and ragged specimen.

For the first time in a long time, anger had its way with Milborne. Firing squad or hangman's rope, either was better than any more of this being cooped up behind five foot thick walls. He figured the odds of ever making it back to the states alive were near zero. He had a bellyful of prison life. And wanted no more of it.

A WEEK PASSED and still no word of being moved again. Late one night, Milborne awoke to hear the cell door creak open on its metal hinges. He did not pop out of bed for fear of getting a rifle buttstock to the face like he'd seen happen to other curious prisoners.

After some grunting and shuffling noises, the door creaked closed again and he was alone. Except that he wasn't.

In the dark quiet, Milborne stole across the small room and confirmed what he suspected. A body, no sounds of breath, now lay on the other cot. It was too dark to see who the dead man might be. Either the guards did not notice they had beaten someone to death, or they just needed a place to put the body before burial. Disgust swelled in Milborne's stomach. In the morning, with the aid of a small shaft of light, he flipped the blanket away from covering the face. It was none other than Miguel. "Those bastards," he uttered in a low growl. To think of the hardship that the young man had endured, and the hopes of being reunited with his family. Never to be.

Milborne knelt and prayed until he heard a

marching outside his cell door. Daylight streamed from down the hall as a man stepped into view. "I am Delgado Estanza, jefe de policía de contado."

HOPE AND LOSS

"*D*o you have questions, senor?" Delgado asked.

"I do. Why would you put a dead man in here with me?"

The Mexican sheriff scratched his greasy double chin. "I assure you, he was alive when he was put in there with you." An evil grin slid across his mouth under the ragged mustache. Then he raised his finger, placing it over his pursed lips. "Ah, you must have killed him then!"

Milborne lunged upward and took hold of the bars, causing the man to take a quick step back. Fear shone through Delgado's face for the briefest of moments, only to be replaced with anger.

"Why are you doing this?" Milborne asked.

"Because you are like my prized Steer," he replied. "You see, there is an American amigo of mine. I help him, and he helps me. Very lucrative with revolution in the air, and the more chaos sure to come."

If the sheriff had been just a few inches closer, Milborne would have shot his hands through the bars and wrapped them around his throat. He imagined the man's breath fizzling out beneath Milborne's own strangling fingers.

"I see you are angry, but do not waste your strength on trying to escape. I will come back for you soon."

After the sheriff left the hallway, a guard approached the cell and stared through the bars at Milborne. Milborne was at his wits' end. He had to try something. "The snake feeds tonight," he said, hoping it might be the man named Hector that he sought. The guard's cool expression did not change in the slightest. He simply turned and walked away.

MILBORNE RETURNED to the body of the dead youth, his heart broken for the innocent youth. Why did they leave the body in the cell with him? Milborne tilted the body to find that a small knife had been driven into the man's back, buried up to the hilt. It was clearly murder, with Milborne as the scapegoat.

After darkness fell, Milborne worked through all that night. Using the knife and his bare fingers, he hacked out a shallow grave in the prison's dirt floor. The surface was hard packed, but underneath lay softer soil he could work with. His calloused hands were bleeding when morning came.

Milborne did not know how Delgado would react when he returned to find an insolent gringo sitting alone in the cell, but it didn't matter. The poor young man needed to be laid to rest, so it had to be done.

The next day, confusion reigned across Delgado's face when he asked, "Where is he?"

"Where is who?" Milborne replied.

Delgado grew into a rage that he was incapable of camouflaging. "I will find him, and when I do..."

An older man, who had followed Delgado, came up to the bars and peered into the cell. He had the air of a gentleman, wearing black muslin pants and a leather fringed vest over his white buttoned up shirt. "I thought you said my son was here? Please, return my money until you can provide him to me." He reached out for a money belt that the sheriff had tightly clutched under one arm.

With his free arm, Delgado waved for another guard, then handed the belt to him. "Take this, and put it somewhere safe," he ordered.

"Where is my son?" The old man insisted. Delgado ignored him, speaking again to the guard holding the belt. "But first, unlock this door."

The guard obeyed. When the door swung open,

Delgado pushed the questioning man inside with Milborne. The guard quickly re-locked the door.

"It doesn't matter now," Delgado said. "Your son, I wanted to return him alive to you, but he died from the long trip here. Now you can take his place. And because you just tried to attack me, I will be able to legally seize your assets."

The old man did not speak. He stood facing the blank wall as if in shock. As soon as the guards left Milborne and Montoya alone, Milborne knew he had to show the man the truth. They unearthed Miguel, then Montoya said his goodbyes. Weeping for the son he almost saved.

INSIDER HELP

*L*ong after dark, a faint shuffling sound outside Milborne's cell awoke him. The lock of the jail door clanked with the sound of being unclasped as a lantern floated beyond the bars. A face Milborne recognized popped into view, the same guard he had spoken the coded sentence to.

"I am in charge until Delgado arrives," Hector said. "You must leave now."

Without making a sound, Milborne and Montoya followed the man down the hall, bypassing several doors until stepping into another room. It was an office lit by several lanterns. Their eerie glow cast many shadows around a table and several chairs.

Hector stopped at a half-height door behind the table. "You must exit this way. You'll find two horses by—"

Two men stepped from the dark doorway of an

adjacent room. "You think I didn't know you've been thwarting me, Hector?" Delgado pointed a pistol at his betrayer. Lit from the lantern light below, his smug face looked almost demon-like. The guard who had accompanied Delgado had his rifle fixated on Milborne. Neither of them bothered to cover Montoya, not seeing the old man as much of a threat.

"Hand over the rifle," Delgado commanded.

"I've had enough of this," Hector said. "You've no right to trade prisoners as bargaining chips." He began the suicide move of slowly raising his rifle to point back at Delgado, but before the sheriff shot him, the sudden glint of a blade flashed in the dim light and struck Delgado in the chest as if it came there by some magic trick.

Delgado let go of his pistol and fell back against the wall.

"That is for killing my Son!" Montoya cried. Milborne recognised the hilt protruding from the sheriff's chest as the same one he had found in Miguel's back.

Milborne and Hector rushed at Delgado's guard. Hector arrived first as the rifle fired, catching him in the leg as he went down. Milborne immobilized the guard soon after, then turned to check on Hector. The man took the pain of being shot as quietly as stubbing a toe. He gave a return look that told Milborne he'd be okay. Next, Milborne bound the downed guard with a short length of police-issued rope already cut to the right size for prisoners' wrists.

They looked over at the now dead Delgado. The smug look on his face was long gone. With help from Milborne and Montoya, Hector found the keys to the safe and opened it. He removed the money belt containing the ten-thousand in American dollars and returned it to Montoya.

The old man held a forlorn look in his eyes as he slung the cash belt over his shoulder, wearing it like a sackcloth of mourning.

"You must go now, before the light," Hector said. He gave a low grunt of pain as he climbed stiffly to his feet, holding his palm tight against the wound at his leg. "There will be more Delgado loyalists arriving soon. They will know you've escaped and be looking for you. Take the two horses outside the livery barn."

"No," Montoya replied, "not without my son."

"I will be sure that he gets a proper burial," Hector assured him.

"No. I am not leaving without him."

"Okay. take the body. But we must hurry... they'll be sending a posse, maybe even two, for you."

They wrapped Miguel's body in a horse blanket and secured it behind Montoya's saddle. "I will be alright," Hector said. "The bullet did not have my name, today. Go now. I will try to right the wrongs that have been committed here."

Milborne and Montoya found the horses and set their escape along a dark trail. Many eager and bloodthirsty men would look for them before too long, Milborne surmised. Montoya for his cash, and himself for the reward his head would bring.

RIDERS IN THE STORM

*M*ilborne and Montoya rode through the rest of the night, and right before dawn they found a place to take shelter. The Canyon directly beneath them cut a deep, jagged scar in the valley floor. Across the vast canyon, the opposite rim looked just like the ridge they were standing on; a red stoned wall of lofty height. Beyond the opposite rim, the land fell away into low rolling hills, carpeted with the indigenous scrub-brush and cactus of the Southwest.

"They won't be far behind," Milborne said.

"Es true," Montoya replied as he scanned the countryside. "But I know the way. We must reach the Río Conchos. It rises high in the Sierra Madre Occidental of Chihuahua. We can follow it to my hacienda... about a hundred and twenty miles from here."

"You want me to go with you?"

"Of course, senor. You'll be safe. They would not look for you so close to the border."

"I want to say yes, but I reckon I should head south."

"Please consider my offer. I am a wealthy man who had so prospered under the rules that Diaz had set, but now I see there must be a change. I know you could be of help to fight the annexation of Mexico into foreign hands."

"You really think you can make a difference?"

"Maybe. But I feel that this power grab by Madero may not last. There could be several more of them in the future. Who knows? But I imagine, years from now, we will have a country united with fairness to all."

Milborne leaned back and covered his face with his hat. It wasn't the nice one he'd had as a Rurales, but this one was Hector's. He'd given it to him when they parted saying he'd need it for their ride. He was right. "Sounds like a pie in the sky idea to me," Milborne said from underneath the hat. "Government ain't so easily changed."

"Only revolution will do," Montoya replied, "but most of the people are too weak in body and will. That's why I need your help."

Milborne removed the hat from his face and took a hard look at Montoya. "I don't know what I could do there, but I will go with you, old man. I owe you for helping me in that unplanned escape. And someone needs to see you back home so's you can get your boy a proper burial."

The sadness in Montoya's face was overwhelming, so much so that Milborne had to avert his eyes. "I have to tell you. When I was out on the trail with Miguel... we covered nearly eight-hundred miles and he helped me get through the worst of it. Heck, he even fed me when they wouldn't untie my hands to eat."

Milborne took a long pause before continuing. "And... when they were beating him. I tried to stop 'em. With all my might, I tried."

"Is that when they killed him?"

"No, we still had a few days more to travel. He was alive when we made it into Delicias. I had a fever by then so they shipped me to the hospital. I assumed I'd see him in the jail afterward." Milborne took a drink of water from a canteen they found on the horse. His mouth dry from all the telling. "He was already gone when they put him in the cell with me."

"Thank you, senor. It's nice to know that he had a friend in the end."

"You know," Milborne said, "I admit maybe I gambled all too often in the past. It's a thankless distraction. I can see how a man can get lost in it."

"Yes. I tried to show my son the good use of his pay, but he would not understand. If I had squandered my money, I never would have been able to build my hacienda."

"It would be nice," Milborne said, "To have my own hacienda, someday." If there ever would be a someday for him, he thought.

Both men were silent after that, feeling that any more words would be useless to convey the fog of heartache and regret looming over them.

CLOUDS ROLLED in as the day progressed. Being the rainy season during a wet spring, nature quit her hoarding of the water supply causing flowers to bloom in swaths of color across the valley. Travel was much slower during daylight as they had to stay hidden as possible. The threat of a posse ambushing them stayed fresh on Milborne's mind.

More clouds rolled in, and with that came a strong wind, heavy rain, and claps of thunder as the sky went dark with the setting sun. They had to keep moving. Milborne followed Montoya as best he could. The old man had picked the Criollo to ride which stood a good fifteen hands high and chosen since he had the extra load of Miguel's body. Milborne had no choice but to take the smaller horse. Before long, Montoya outpaced them, trudging across the treacherous landscape until crossing a muddy wash. That's when Milborne's horse went down.

A SHOCKING DISCOVERY

*A*fter scrambling around in the dark mud with the howling wind above, Milborne pulled hard on the saddle horn until getting re-saddled and upright again. By then Montoya was no longer in sight. He looked for tracks, but the rain had easily washed them away.

The stormy night ticked on as Milborne did his best to go in the direction where he believed Montoya to be. The river... he had to find the river. But no sense going on until the worst of it passed. Besides, he couldn't see the stars to save his life, so navigating the unfamiliar territory was pointless. He found an outcropping of rock to shield him from the rain and waited till morning.

~

With the light of day came a shocking discovery. Montoya's money belt lashed to his horse. Milborne didn't remember when it happened, yet there it was. Why would Montoya have done it? By mistake or on purpose? It didn't matter. Here he was, alone and packing ten-thousand dollars of the man's money.

Milborne mounted and sat at the crossroads of his mind. Did Montoya really need all that money? The man was a wealthy landowner and wouldn't miss it. Milborne had said that he'd see him safely back home, but Montoya knew his way much better than he. Heck, Milborne deserved that money after all he went through in his life. No, he hadn't robbed that bank back in El Paso, but the bank manager was in on the scam and even hinted he could use Milborne's kindly assistance. Despite rejecting the offer, they still blamed him for a crime he did not commit. Maybe it'd be best to blaze a trail south. The cash would get him through with the bribes he would surely have to make along the way.

Milborne never considered himself a deceitful man, but he'd been so when the times warranted. Why was this such a tough decision now? Why a conscience should remain when all else was gone, he could only guess. "Oh hell's-bells-son-of-a-gun-and-dadgummit!" He shouted to the heavens. If he were to take the money as his own, then he'd be doing the same thing that the corrupt officials of the government were doing. Stealing the blood and sweat of a

livelihood from another. He slew his horse north-
ward and dug heels into its sides.

He had a handle on the right thing to do now,
and a powerful hope that he would find Montoya
before the posse did.

A DOG IN THE NIGHT

*T*he sky cleared as Milborne stopped to rest on rolling hills of scrub and agave so common in the Chihuahuan desert. It was a diverse place with broad desert basins bordered by mesas and mountain ranges. The smell, though. He'd always loved the fresh scent of the desert after a heavy rain. The newness of it all. As if the past somehow didn't matter, offering a man the chance to start anew. With luck, he'd hit the river soon, and that would surely guide him to the hacienda of Montoya.

Milborne considered camping for the night, a bright moon hanging above him. He could have made a fire. All it took was a little extra work; his father had taught him that. But no, he had to keep moving. The sad cry of a coyote echoed across the night. If it got hungry enough, he may have some trouble yet. And he knew they hunted in a pack to gain an advantage over larger prey. Even a man on a horse didn't guarantee safety when it came to the prairie wolf's tenacity.

He reached a hill and checked his back-trail. A campfire lay in the far distance. It must be the posse. How blatant to burn such a large flame. It had to be his pursuers.

As Milborne started on his way in the northwesterly direction of the river, he felt as if someone, something, were watching him. A soft snap beyond the range of his limited vision confirmed a suspicion that coyotes were most likely advancing through the trees. He withdrew the pistol Hector had given him for defense, glad to have it. Slowly, he backtracked in such a way to get behind his canine followers, hopefully getting one up on them from the flank to make em' scatter.

"Hey, Milborne."

The human voice coming from the darkness directly ahead of him. Nearly caused his heart to stop. Ramirez.

The man stepped out into the yellowish glow of moonlight. He wore no hat, making it look like he had a skull for a face; the shadows casting sinister caves for his eyes. "I'd heard you escaped, so I hitched up with the posse over yonder. They was too damn slow, so I left them back aways. Must be my lucky night."

"You won't take me alive, Ramirez."

"Suits me. I've taken you down once. I can do so again."

Ramirez flew from the shadows in a surprise lunge.

Milborne blocked the knife with his forearm but the body-slam hit him with the force of a bull and down they went. After breaking free from an attempted wrestling hold, Milborne scrambled to a nearby boulder. He thought it had hidden him well enough in the darkness, but Ramirez must've had a bead on him and thumbed a bullet. It ricocheted off stone mere inches away so Milborne rolled away and into a dark gully. Turning, the luck of the new position gave him a clear shot. He didn't want to kill the man, but he had the right to defend himself in a situation that would most likely lead to his death.

"Come on, Milborne, let's face each other like real—"

Milborne squeezed the trigger and watched as the man's six-gun flew out of his hand. Milborne was no gunfighter, so he was surprised as a couple of Ramirez's fingers disappeared along with it.

Ramirez shrieked like a banshee as he cradled the hand near his body. Milborne took his chance and hightailed it away and into the night. He doubted the posse had heard the gunshots being far away as they were. The ridgeline between them would have helped muffle the reports as well. Still, he had to make haste and get as far away as he could. He found his horse but a few feet away and once again rode for his life.

Two days of the hardest riding he'd ever done, and at last Milborne reached the river. Now all he had to do was follow it North as Montoya said it would lead him right to the hacienda. Hours later, he spied something ahead. A short mile away there curled a wispy column of smoke which bespoke of habitation. The hacienda, he'd found it.

When he got closer, though, he found it well hidden. Deep in a narrow valley with sheer rock walls enclosing it. From high on the ridge on which he now stood, the place looked much smaller than he imagined. Either Montoya really knew how to exaggerate his status in life, or it was the wrong place.

Still, he had to approach and see who lived there. If it was indeed the wrong place, at least he might get directions. Was he ready for this, though? He wore the stamp of the hunted as naturally as he wore the dust of the great desert he had just crossed. How would he pull off this first encounter with civilized humanity? Simply walking up to a door and knocking seemed absurd.

At least the sun had burnt some of the pallor out

of his arms and hands. And the incessant riding had done much to put back the tone in long inactive muscle. But any resemblance to the Rurales captain he'd been was ended. Milborne didn't want to ride the horse right up to the front door, so he secured him in a nestle of trees and made his way into the canyon.

The hot and brassy noon-day sun dogged Milborne for the duration of his descent from the top of the ridge. The gaining of each foothold was a dangerous affair. There must've been an easier path down, one that his smaller horse, a Galiceno he guessed, could travel. But this wasn't it.

Thread-bare clothing hung loose on his body. Black hair now hung to his shoulders. He didn't need a mirror to see the rough beginnings of a beard on his chin. His tall, gaunt frame moved with the guarded actions of one long used to exercising his right to self-preservation. Old habits are not easily erased. He tried to practice a smile, but it did little to ease the hardness of his mouth; around which hovered the grimness of long and solitary suffering.

In the end, he thought, it was better that he'd come across this small homestead first, instead of a massive hacienda. Milborne was versed enough in the local customs to know that one did not burst in upon the rich tradition-enslaved Hidalgo's without first gaining permission for an audience. Even if he had already met the master of the house.

As though to reassure himself, he felt for the sweat laden money belt he'd carried since separating from Montoya. The long mound of U.S. Paperbacks clung as a weighty burden in more ways than one. Many times during the past weeks he had almost changed course for parts unknown. Even though Milborne had his fill of sun and baking alkali encrusted ground beneath his boots, an unknown pull from deep inside had kept him from straying further south.

He shrugged, as though by doing so he could throw off the ghosts of his past. He forced himself to attend to the business at hand. He knocked on the front door.

A BRIEF RESPITE

A woman eased the door open. The look on her face was one of surprise, but not fear. "I see you are not the Federales I've been expecting," she said.

"Uh, no Mamm, I'm not." Milborne took off his hat and held it in his hands. "I'm really wanting to find senor Motoya's hacienda, he's a good friend of mine." Milborne caught himself in a white lie. He was not a good friend, but he liked Montoya and thought maybe there would be the chance of a friendship barring a gravestone for either of them.

She opened the door wider, "Please senor, come in."

The comfort of the minimal living space astonished Milborne. Anejlita was not wealthy, but she made the home a most gracious and welcoming place.

"Are you hungry?" she asked.

Milborne's stomach rumbled. The hard-tack had run out a while ago, and had little time for hunting for food. The smell of something cooking in the kitchen wafted by.

"Please sit here at the table. It's nearly two o'clock so you must have a traditional comida with me before getting on your way."

The meal started with a large glass of rice milk and warm albondigas soup, followed by a healthy heaping of bright orange colored Spanish rice. Milborne did his best for manners, but it wasn't easy when the main course came along. The massive plate of enchiladas was flooded with red chile sauce and mounds of cheese. Alongside were chopped onions, lettuce, and some eggs which were most likely cooked in hot lard. The colorful fare bursting with spice. Pungent flavors nearly overwhelming a man who'd been on such a basic diet.

When Milborne had the rarefied feeling of a satisfied stomach, Anjelita told him about how her husband left to fight for freedom from the long impositions of the corrupt government. It had been more than a month and the man still hadn't sent word back that he was still okay. Her prospects now lay in the form of having a Federale come to the door and tell her that her husband might be captured, or worse.

She confirmed that she knew of the hacienda of

Montoya. He was indeed wealthy, but his estate was unique in that Montoya built it himself; not on the backs of the locals like many other plantations had done as they flourished during the corrupt Diaz regime. Those truly massive haciendas with their impressive arches, petite balconies and peach-colored walls kept people in debt and toiling on the same piece of land that once was theirs or their families.

Milborne left the house and went up to the ridge to retrieve his horse. Once he led the animal down a path safely back to the house, it finally got some feed and a good watering. After Anjelita gave him directions, Milborne climbed back into the saddle with the strength of a new man. He crossed his forearms on the saddle horn and asked, "Might I risk getting shot since I won't be able to announce myself before stepping onto his land?"

"I know senor Montoya," she replied. "He is no hacendado. Those types of landlords simply take more land and existing villages by force, using them as they please. Don't worry, he will have men on the vast acreage out looking for you." Her expression turned to one of deep concern. "Will the corruption of our government ever end?"

"Yes," Milborne said, "but only if people like senor Montoya use their resources to make it happen." He bid Anjelita farewell, once again thanking her for her hospitality. The likes of which he hadn't seen for years. A long-lost smile washed over him as he rode away.

Continuing for several miles, many more than matching what Anjelita had specified, Milborne thought maybe he wasn't headed in the right direction. Caution rang in Milborne's befuddled mind. What if he'd gone too far? It'd be a damn shame to accidentally waltz across the border and into some waiting gallows.

SOMEONE IN NEED

"*A*yúdame! Ayúdame, por favor!"

Milborne heard the cry coming from over the next hill. Was it a trap? It sounded like a child, but the idea of a trap crossed his mind. A minute later he came upon a boy lying up against a rock. The child couldn't have been more than eight years old.

"Estoy gravemente herida senor. Me puedes ayudar?"

Milborne had little fluency of the Spanish language, but knew enough to understand that the boy had been calling for help. After spending a few moments in a quick circle of the area to assure that it was safe, he returned to the boy and asked, "Where are you hurt?"

The boy did not speak. Instead, he removed his hand from a part of his ankle, obviously protecting a purplish welt. Milborne followed the child's eyes to see the smashed body of a large scorpion nearby.

Maybe the boy was exploring and became lost. There were many times when as a child, Milborne ventured out on his own back in New York, bored with the city and restless to explore the less populated surroundings. He could not fault the boy one iota. "Mi nombre es Milborne," he said.

"Beto," the boy replied.

Beto could not stand, let alone walk on his own. But Milborne couldn't leave him to die alone. Soon the poison would work its way to the chest and might even stop his heart. He used some leather scrap from the saddlebag and made a tourniquet just above the wound. Beto grimaced in pain, but he did not cry out.

"You're a tough little hombre," Milborne said.

Beto smiled through his pain.

No choice now but to head back to Anjelita's for help. He didn't have time to wander around looking for Montoya's place. That would have to wait. He lifted Beto onto the horse and they rode. The going went smoothly until he jerked on the reins, ducking the horse into a wash. "Dammit all!" he whispered. It was the posse.

Ramirez might have rejoined them, but Milborne wasn't sure whether they blocked his path intentionally, or by accident. The choices were not getting any easier, and more complex with the added difficulty of having the boy. For he was now Milborne's charge, his responsibility. They took off at a full gallop away from the posse. Either he would find Montoya's place, or run straight across the border and into a hanging.

"Just try and hold on, compadre," Milborne said. They descended a rough incline and made their way across a sun soaked valley buzzing with desert life. As he slowed his mount to navigate a rocky outcropping, a shot rang through the air. His horse collapsed underneath and down they went.

OUT OF THE FRYING PAN

Someone in the posse had a lousy aim or didn't care about killing a horse. The poor beast was dead. In Milborne's book, it was the shooter who should be hanged. Beto was thrown clear, but Milborne's foot had become pinned under the horse's side. He worked his ankle free and skipped over to the boy. He was no worse for wear, so Minore scooped him up and took off on foot. The posse had indeed caught up with him.

Sweat poured into Milborne's eyes as he tried to keep an all-out run. Zigzagging to help from being shot. This boy was a stranger, so why did he feel so much more important than that? He heard once that most folks are naturally inclined to protect someone else with a greater fierceness than even defending their own life. And now Milborne was taking care of the child as if he were his own.

Milborne tripped. He stumbled down an embankment and landed on top of a cactus bush but still held onto his charge. Pain seared his right thigh as he lifted himself free. Instead of a run, he could only maintain a lopsided motion to keep moving. This was it. He probably wouldn't make it. Maybe Beto would be spared, he did not know. They'd take Milborne, though, and punish him for being so free spirited.

Up ahead he spied a cliff edge with a great canyon beyond. He'd have to take his chances, no matter how long a fall there might be. More shots rang out, exploding a tall cactus behind. He skidded to the canyon edge and looked down. The ground sloped away at a steep angle for at least fifty yards, ending in a vast swath of thornbush. He jumped.

Milborne slid down the gravelly slope on his ass while maintaining a sitting up position. With each bump, the cactus needles pushed deeper into Milborne's leg. Still, he clutched the boy close, as if he were the most valuable treasure he'd ever found. After coming to a stop, covered with dust and having lost his hat, Milborne ducked into the brush and began looking for an exit to crawl through. He felt like a wild animal on the run.

After some entanglements, Milborne popped out the prickly thornbush and stood tall, ready to start running again, but a new sight stopped him dead in his tracks. A short distance ahead stood a group of men atop their horses. It wasn't the posse. Rather, he knew all too well the look of the United States Texas Rangers. Holding Beto in his arms, he fell to his knees. His breathing staggered and strength nearly gone, he had no choice but to surrender to them.

Milborne never would have imagined that the Rangers would be the ones to pull him out of the quagmire he'd gotten himself into. They took the boy and tied Milborne's hands together. After one of the Rangers relieved Milborne of his cash burden, the posse of Delgado loyalists appeared at the top of the ridge. After a few minutes they reappeared on a lower side trail which was not as steep as the one Milborne and Beto had came down.

As the posse came to a stop in front of them, Milborne eyed each one, but Ramirez was not with them. Hopefully still searching for his lost fingers. The leader of the posse came forward and argued his case to take Milborne. The man wanted his fugitive badly, but he maintained an air of respect to the Ranger captain. It was purported that some rangers wouldn't hesitate to lynch Mexicans and Mexican Americans along the Texas-Mexico border. In the end, the Rangers made it clear that Milborne and the boy belonged to them. Dejected, the angry mob rode away. For all their troubles, getting nothing in return.

After Milborne's leg was tended to, the trip across the border to El Paso first took them up to the Rio Grande, then they followed it toward the northwest. They were both fed well along the way, but the rangers kept to themselves and did not ask Milborne questions. That wasn't their job. He almost asked what would happen to him, but he did not want the answer they might provide. They were kind enough to treat Beto for the poison, and he improved soon after.

THE EL PASO facility was much cleaner than any Mexican jail Milborne had ever seen, and he'd seen a lot of them both inside and out. Now it looked as if he'd see a lot more, just on the American side. Before an eventual execution that is. A few excruciating days went by while Milborne waited for his fate, until a familiar figure appeared outside the bars.

"I guess this is what the French call a... Deja Vu?" Milborne asked.

"Yes. It is, my friend." Montoya replied. "As this is how I find you, yet again. But I am glad you are safe."

"Safe? I'm due for a hanging any day now. How in tarnation did you track me down?"

"A woman, Anjelita. She was kind enough to tell me what happened, and where you were headed. I thought you knew how to navigate this territory?"

Milborne felt slightly offended. "Well, it's been a few years since I came down through these parts.

But believe me, when on the run, you don't take long to admire the scenery."

Montoya chuckled. "I understand. And besides, the border patrol are some tough vaqueros. They hunt and catch fugitives on both sides of the border, daily. Maybe in a hundred years someone might build a massive wall instead."

"Never going to happen," Milborne replied. He sat on the hard metal bench and ran both hands over his face and up through his hair. "Look, I've been thinking about that bank manager here in El Paso. The one who asked me to help with the robbery? I'm wondering if he might've been the one who framed me for the murder of that teller. I think he may be Delgado's contact here. I think—"

"It's okay. I already found him. Hector has been helping me work with the American authorities who are not corrupt. That man has been rooted out and his many other schemes discovered."

"Does that mean?"

"Yes, my friend... you are a free man in a free country."

After Montoya conferred with the warden for a few moments, a jailer walked up to the door and twisted a key into the lock until finding a loud click. The door swung wide.

TIME TO MOVE ON

*A*fter Milborne claimed his crumpled hat, the only possession besides the clothes on his back, he stepped out into the warm daylight. The jail sat near the edge of town with a widening valley of trees as the backdrop. A row of beautiful mountains lay beyond. He took in a deep breath of the fresh morning air, releasing it slowly.

Montoya stepped up alongside. "I wanted to thank you for returning the money they tried to steal from me." Montoya handed him an envelope of paper secured with string.

Milborne unwrapped it to see it was the same money he had been traveling with. "I.. I can't take this."

"No, it is yours, now. My way of thanking you for helping me bring home my son. It cannot bring him back, but you can use it to maybe start your own hacienda."

Milborne felt a welling of tears, but he nonchalantly wiped them aside with the back of his hand and faked a small cough. "It has been a long, long ride."

"Life is a long ride, my friend."

"I would've liked to see your hacienda," Milborne said.

"Oh, it is a grande place. I am lucky to have such sprawling and fertile land. And you are always welcome."

"No, thank you, just the same. I'd prefer to stay on this side of the border from here on out."

Milborne lifted the envelope holding the bundle of American dollars in his hand, "Thank you for this," he said, then he tucked it into his belt. "How do you know I won't give in to temptation and just gamble it all away?"

"You would not do such a thing."

Milborne knew his friend was right, for he was already thinking of a more sensible plan. "I will use it wisely. But how can I thank you for gaining my freedom?"

"You can keep doing what you've been doing. Fight for others' freedom, as well as your own. We've both been victims of abuse by our government's people who carry out their misdeeds from high places. I will continue to root them out in my own country. You know," Montoya paused to scratch his chin, "I have a cousin named Pancho, and he lives over in Chihuahua. He's been saying that change is needed, and he is an ombre of action. I will have to see if he would fight for Mexico along with me."

"What of Beto," Milborne asked. "The boy I found while looking for you?"

"He is well. I am taking him back with me. He was hunting to provide his family with a meal. Lucky you found him."

"I am." Milborne thought back to the decision he made to rescue the boy, knowing that regardless, it was the right one.

Montoya held out his hand, "Well, good luck to you."

Milborne returned the man's firm grip, knowing that he indeed found a friend.

As Milborne went on his way, taking a slow walk into town, he thought about how much smaller it all felt now. El Paso had grown, but then so had he. His long ride across the great country of Mexico was the toughest time in his life, but it showed him that there can be a better future, if he wanted it.

Staying in El Paso, though, was not what he wanted. Time for a new life. But where? He'd heard that some of the northern states were just begging for people to settle up there. One thing for sure; he wanted to be far away from the Mexican border.

Milborne set out for the great state of Wyoming,

figuring that maybe he'd build a ranch there. Maybe even set down roots. A hacienda he could call his own. And with some extra good luck, meet a woman who might cook like Anjelita.

THE END

www.ingramcontent.com/pod-product-compliance
Lightning Source LLC
Chambersburg PA
CBHW020641130626
46552CB00003B/1340